COLLINGWOOD O'HARE ENTERTAINMENT LTD

First published 2002 by Walker Books Ltd

87 Vauxhall Walk, London SE11 5HJ

2 4 6 8 10 9 7 5 3 1

Based on the animated series "Eddy & the Bear"

Series developed by Tony Collingwood and Helen Stroud

Produced by Christopher O'Hare

© 2002 Collingwood O'Hare Entertainment Ltd

Printed and bound in Great Britain by Ebenezer Bayliss Ltd

British Library Cataloguing in Publication Data:

a catalogue record for this book is available

from the British Library

ISBN 0-7445-8975-4

Eddy & the Bear in

The Best Things in Life

From the original script by Tony Collingwood

WALKER BOOKS
AND SUBSIDIARIES
LONDON • BOSTON • SYDNEY

Eddy and his mum were hard at work painting the house.

"Mum," said Eddy, "what do I get for helping?"

Mum thought hard. "How about ... a kiss and a cuddle?"

Eddy giggled. "Aw, Mum!" he said. "I don't want that mushy stuff. Can I have some more pocket money instead?"

"Oh, Eddy," said Mum. "You've had your pocket money this week."

"I know," said Eddy sheepishly. "But I've spent it already."

Later, Eddy went to the wood to talk to his best friend, Bear.

"What am I going to do, Bear?" said Eddy. "My friends at school can buy lots of games and toys, but I can't. I need money!"

"You need a bunny?" replied Bear. "Don't worry, Eddy. I know a bunny called George."

Eddy laughed. "Silly! I said 'money', not 'bunny'! All the best things cost *money.*"

"But Eddy," said Bear, "what about the things that are free?"

"Huh! If it doesn't cost at least *this* much" – Eddy stretched his arms out wide – "then it's just *boring.*"

"Hmm…" said Bear, scratching his head thoughtfully.

That night it rained and rained, but by the morning the sky was clear and the sun was shining. Eddy put on his wellies and went to find Bear, splashing in all the puddles along the way.

"Eddy!" called Bear. "What are you doing?"

"I'm splashing in the puddles with my yellow wellies!" Eddy shouted. "Whee!"

"Well, you shouldn't be!" said Bear. "Can't you see the price tags?"

Eddy looked around. Bear had stuck a twig into the ground next to each and every puddle. And every twig had a leaf, just like a price tag.

Bear looked serious. "Splashing in puddles costs money, Eddy. This puddle here costs" – Bear stretched his arms out wide – "this much!"

"But ... but I don't have any money," said Eddy sadly.

"No?" said Bear. "Well, that means you can't splash in puddles, or blow dandelions, or climb the big oak tree."

"Wait a minute, Bear!" said Eddy. "*You* don't have any money either! You'll have to get a job."

"Me? Get a job?" asked Bear. "Like what?"

Eddy tried to imagine what a bear like Bear could do for a job. "Let's see..." said Eddy slowly. "Maybe you could be ... I know! An *astronaut*..."

"I think I'd rather just be a bear,
   please," said Bear, as they lay back
   looking up at the sky.

"Being a bear isn't a job, silly!"
   said Eddy.

"But I'm very good at it," said Bear.
"See? I'm doing it right now."

Suddenly Eddy stood
up. "I've just thought
of the perfect job
for you!" he said.
"But we have to ask
   Mum. Come on!
   Let's go back to my house!"

"Mum!" called Eddy. "Bear needs a job! Can he paint the rest of the house?"

"House painting is not a job for a bear," said Mum. "Sorry, Bear."

"But I need the money, Mrs Eddy," said Bear.

"Well, if you want to help, you can carry in the shopping," said Mum. "The car's full – all the shops in town are having their summer sales."

In a flash, Eddy got the best idea yet. "That's it!" he cried. "That's the answer!"

"What?" said Bear excitedly.

"You know all the things in the wood that we can't afford?" said Eddy. "We'll lower the prices. We'll have a summer sale!"

Bear gasped. "That's brilliant, Eddy! So how much should we charge to splash in puddles and to blow dandelions and to climb the big oak tree?"

"Nothing!" cried Eddy. "As of right now, puddle-splashing is free! Dandelion-blowing is free! And big-oak-tree-climbing is ab-so-lute-ly ... freeeee!"

Bear was amazed. "That *is* cheap!" he exclaimed, as he splashed in a great big puddle.
"So everything is free?"

"Yes," said Eddy, splashing along beside him.
"Especially all the *best* things."

Then Eddy and Bear laughed and laughed – because, of course ... that was free too.

Jez Alborough says,

"Eddy & the Bear books are all about friendship. Wouldn't we all like to have a friend like Bear? One who is silly and fun, but also kind and loving. When you have a friend like that, everything you do together becomes an adventure. Each Eddy & the Bear book captures one of their adventures – so we can all join in!"

Jez Alborough has written and illustrated numerous children's picture books, including **Cuddly Dudley, Watch Out! Big Bro's Coming!**, **Hug** and the three original stories about Eddy and the Bear: **Where's My Teddy?**, **It's the Bear!** and **My Friend Bear**.

ISBN 0-7445-3058-X (pb)

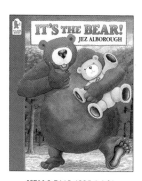

ISBN 0-7445-4385-1 (pb)

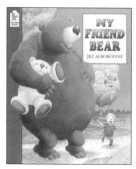

ISBN 0-7445-6918-4 (pb)

Look out for more books based on the popular animated TV series Eddy & the Bear!